RACER BUDDIES

OPENING DAY AT DAYTONA!

written by **Craig Elliott**

illustrated by **William A. Harper**

art direction & graphic design by **Dale Engelbert & Susan Szymanski**

NASCAR ® is a registered trademark of the National Association for Stock Car Auto Racing, Inc.

DAYTONA ®, Daytona International Speedway ®, North Carolina Speedway ® and The Rock ™
are used under license from International Speedway Corporation

GOODYEAR ® (the winged foot design) and EAGLE ®
are used with permission of The Goodyear Tire & Rubber Company

Library of Congress Control Number: 2004100046

ISBN: 0-9746445-0-1

Printed in the United States of America

www.racerbuddies.com

For Adam and Wesley, my racer buddies,
and Lisa, my beautiful wife
who gave them to me.

- Craig Elliott

Bonnie and I would like to
dedicate these illustrations
to each one of our 20 grandchildren.

- William A. Harper

Opening day at Daytona International Speedway was in two days and the Racer Buddies were ready to go. Each Racer wanted a turn to practice on the world famous Daytona track.

"Wow, who was that?" exclaimed Ace, last year's racing champion.

"I could hardly see him when he went by!" said Spark, one of the hardworking Racer Buddies.

"That was Snap, a hot shot **rookie**. I'll teach him a thing or two," sneered Slip. Slip always liked to cause trouble.

"Oh, boy! Daytona is nothing like my little track in Virginia," worried Tuck, as he looked around the huge **infield** and giant **banked turns**. "I don't think I'm ready."

"You'll be fine," smiled Ace, the oldest of the bunch. "Everybody has to have their first big race. Mine was a long time ago, but I felt just as scared as you do today. Let me show you where to go to get ready for your **practice laps**."

"Thanks," said Tuck, although he was still shaking a little inside.

The next day was **qualifying day**, a chance for the cars to show their stuff by being timed for their fastest single **lap**. The Racer Buddies' top times were posted on the scoreboard to show where they would start in the big race.

The cars and their crews worked to make the last adjustments out on the track. The pressure was on. All of the cars were nervous, including last year's champion, Ace. Even he needed a fast qualifying time to make the race.

The Racer Buddies entered Daytona to start their qualifying laps. Even on a qualifying day, the stands were filled with fans as far as you could see.

"Look at all these people! There are more here than in my whole town, maybe my whole state!" exclaimed a wide-eyed Tuck.

"Daytona only seats 165,000 screaming fans. Nothing to be nervous about, Tuck," teased Slip.

Slip was right, the track at Daytona is so large it has a lake built in the infield! The banks in the turns are so steep that a car has to be going at least 70 miles per hour around the corners just so they don't slide down to the infield.

Snap revved his engine in frustration. He wanted out of the pits and onto the track.

"Come on, you guys," said Snap, "I'm ready to rock!"

"Your turn will come," Ace said as he looked around at Snap. "It's a long season and this is just the first race."

"I don't need your help," snapped Snap.

Ace pulled out for his turn and took the first few banked corners nice and easy, checking for the best traction so his racing tires would "stick." Each lap was faster than the last until he found the right place on the track and the right speed to get the fastest lap time of the day.

"Nice lap, Ace!" yelled Tuck.

"Do you think he's done this before?" Spark smiled at the other cars.

"Once or twice, I bet," laughed Tuck.

Ace, the old pro, took an easy lap to cool down and came into the infield as Snap revved up his engine, ready to go.

It was Snap's turn. He smoked his tires out of the pits and onto the track.

"Save your tires, Snap!" yelled Ace. "That won't make you faster, just louder."

"I know what I'm doing," boasted Snap as he flew out of pit row and down the first straightaway.

"Careful, Snap!" radioed his crew chief as Snap slid around the first corner.

Snap made the corner, and it looked like his next lap would be a good one.

"Look at his time!" snarled Slip. "I can't believe that kid is in the lead!"

Snap came sliding sideways across the finish line with a time just faster than Ace's.

"Looks like you have the **pole position**, Snap," said Ace. Ace had seen fast rookies before and wasn't too worried. He knew that a good qualifying lap didn't always mean a good race the next day.

"That was awesome!" yelled Snap.

"Getting the 'pole' is great," warned Ace, "but tomorrow is a 500-mile race and you can't win if you don't finish."

"Yeah, yeah, yeah," snipped Snap.

He didn't want advice from Ace.

On opening day at Daytona the crowd was louder than the cars. The Racer Buddies lined up on the grid behind Pace, the **pace car**, in the order of their qualifying times.

Snap couldn't contain himself. "Come on, Pace! Out of the way, let's GO!"

"Cool it, Snap, I'm in charge here," demanded Pace.

The pace car was always in charge and didn't leave the track until he was convinced that all the cars were in their positions and behaving.

When everyone was in line, Pace signaled to the starter that this was the green flag lap.

"Good luck, Racers!" Pace yelled as he drove off the track and into the pits.

As the cars approached the starting line, the green flag dropped and away they went!

Ace, Spark, and Tuck warmed up their tires over the first few laps and increased their speed gradually. Snap shot out of the grid and started skidding around the first few corners.

"Snap, save your tires," radioed Snap's crew chief, "It's a long race." But Snap was already burning rubber down Daytona's mile-long, Superstretch straightaway.

In the middle of the pack, Slip started to squeeze Tuck up against the wall.

"How's it going there, buddy boy?" snickered Slip.

"Hey, watch it!" whimpered Tuck.

The two racers tore down the straightaway at incredible speeds. Tuck's left door was just inches away from Slip and his right door inches away from the wall.

Tuck took a deep breath and held his line as the two cars went through the corner side by side. Tuck knew he had to put his fears aside if he was going to be a real **NASCAR** racer.

He thought of his old track in Viriginia and how he knew each turn and groove. He loved driving there and remembered how much fun racing could be.

"Look at all those people, Tuck. How are you feeling now?" taunted Slip as he gave Tuck a little bump on his door.

"I'm feeling like a racer!" smiled Tuck as he looked away from the grandstands, away from Slip, and back down at the track ahead.

Tuck remembered what he loved – racing!

Tuck gave Slip a bump, cut down in front of him on the corner, and Slip fell to the back of the pack.

The Racer Buddies went a little faster each lap as they got used to the track. Snap held the lead for the first few laps, but had to stop for his crew to give him more **racing fuel** and four new tires.

While Snap came in for a **pit stop**, the other cars kept going. Their tires weren't worn out and they still had plenty of gas. The other Buddies were driving fast, but not wild, like Snap!

"Hurry up!" Snap yelled to his crew chief.

Snap's crew hurried to get him back on the track but his lead was cut because the other cars didn't have to stop.

Ace moved up to second place.

"I'm coming through, Snap!" said Ace.

"No way, Ace. I'm keeping the lead!" hollered Snap. But once again Snap's rough driving had worn his tires and he didn't have enough **traction** to hold the **racing line** on the inside of the track.

Ace, Spark and Tuck had driven a fast, smart race. They dove down to the inside of the corner and all passed Snap as he slid wide once again.

"What's wrong? I can't hold the line!" barked Snap into his radio.

"You don't have enough tires left!" his crew chief radioed back, but it was too late.

Snap started slipping to the **high side** of the track as his worn tires slid on the track.

"Yahooo!" yelled Ace excitedly as he crossed the finish line in first place.

Spark and Tuck followed in second and third place, and Snap limped across the finish line in fourth place, out of gas and with worn tires.

"Great race, Buddies," Spark said to Ace and Tuck. "You drove fast and remembered to save your tires and gas for the whole race."

"That's the way to win," said Ace.

The first race of the season was over. The Racer Buddies and their crews were packing up and getting ready for the next race.

"Congratulations, Tuck! You got your confidence back and did great on your first race at Daytona. Keep practicing and you might be leading me into the winner's circle next time," Ace smiled.

"Thanks, Ace," said Tuck.

"And Snap, you're going to be a great racer, too," continued Ace. "But you have to remember to think about the whole game. In baseball, it's nine innings. In football, it's four quarters. In racing you have to be fast the whole race, not just one or two laps, if you want to win."

"That's great advice," sighed Snap.

"Not bad for a couple of rookies," smiled Ace. "See you in North Carolina at **The Rock**."

RACING GLOSSARY

Banked Turn The corners that have been built higher on the outside edge than on the inside to allow racers to turn at very high speeds.

Crew Chief The head of the mechanics and race strategy of the team.

Green Flag The flag used to start and restart the race.

High Side The outside edge of the track.

Infield The area inside the circle of the track.

Lap One trip around the track.

NASCAR National Association for Stock Car Auto Racing.

Pace Car An official car that leads the racers around the track to prepare them for the start.

Pit Stop When the racers pull off the track into a special area where the mechanics can give them more gas, change tires, and fix broken parts.

Pole Position   The front row on the inside of the first turn awarded to the racer with the fastest qualifying time.

Practice Laps   Laps the racers are allowed to run to get ready for the upcoming race.

Qualifying Day   The day before the race where racers try to make their best lap time alone to see who will get to race the next day and what order they will start in.

Racing Fuel   Special high performance, 110 octane gasoline used for NASCAR racing.

Racing Line   The fastest path around the track.

Rookie   The name for a first-year racer that competes in a new division.

The Rock   North Carolina Speedway at Rockingham (The Rock), North Carolina.

Traction   The grip that the tires have on the track. This determines how fast a racer can turn before the car starts to slide.

Look for the Racer Buddies'
next adventure
as they travel to
Rockingham, North Carolina to
"Race at the Rock"!